This Bob the Builder Annual belongs to

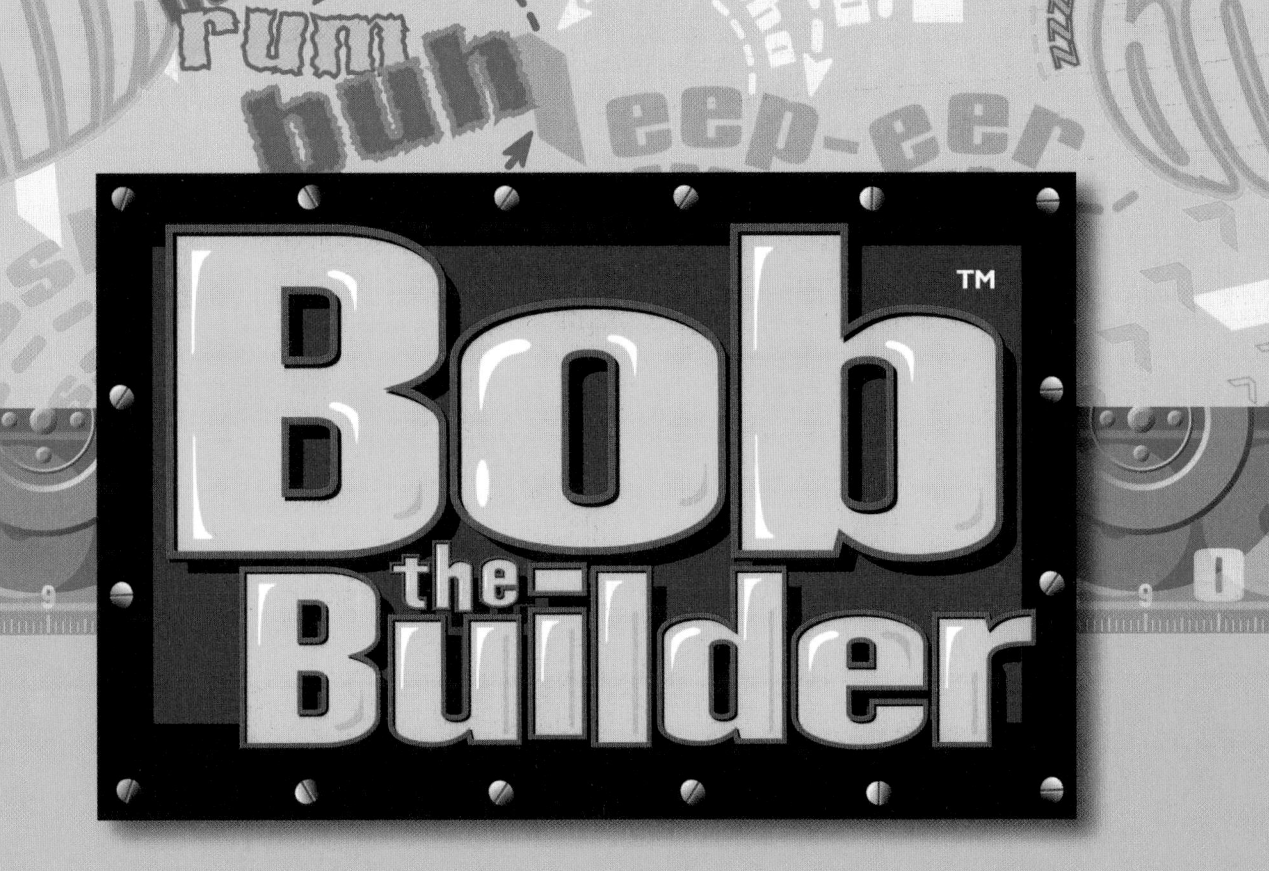

Annual 2006

Contents

Stories adapted from original scripts by James Henry, Jimmy Hibbert, Diane Redmond and Peter Reeves.
Based upon the television series Bob the Builder © HIT Entertainment PLC and Keith Chapman 2005
With thanks to HOT Animation

EGMONT
We bring stories to life
Published in Great Britain in 2005 by Egmont Books Limited,
239 Kensington High Street, London W8 6SA. Printed in Italy. ISBN 1 4052 2043 0
1 3 5 7 9 10 8 6 4 2

"The fun is in getting it done!"

Say hello to Bob and his team

"Can we build it? Yes we can."

Bob the Builder does all sorts of building and mending jobs, from fixing barn roofs to putting up the Christmas tree outside the town hall. Bob loves his job, but he also enjoys line dancing, running and music.

"Let's get to work!"

Wendy is Bob's partner in the building yard – and his best friend. She keeps the office in order, and makes sure that Bob and the team always have all the right tools and equipment. She's a great bricklayer, too.

"No prob, Bob."

Scoop, the big digger, is the leader of Bob's team, and the one Bob can rely on to dig holes or move dirt around. He works hard, but when the job's done he likes to play tricks and tell jokes, too.

"Let's rock and roll!"

Roley is a steamroller who uses his big rollers to smooth and flatten out roads and dirt. He loves making up his own songs and singing them.

"Brilliant!"

Dizzy the cement mixer is the youngest member of Bob's team. She's very lively, and is always chatting and giggling. She loves listening to pop music on her headphones – and playing football!

"Er ... yeah ... I think so."

Lofty is a mobile crane who has three special tools – a grabber, an electro-magnet and a demolition ball. He's a bit nervous and some things scare him, like mice, loud noises and Spud the scarecrow.

"Toot!"

Bird is Roley's best friend. She likes sitting on his roof and singing with him.

"Muck to the rescue."

Muck is a hard-working digger-dumper who likes digging, dumping and moving things around. He loves getting messy and mucky, and there's only one thing he doesn't like – the dark!

"Miaow!"

Pilchard, Bob's cat, is very good at sleeping, watching TV and eating fish. She only speaks "cat", but Bob and his team always seem to know just what she's saying.

Would you like to be part of Bob's team? Draw your picture, then write your name on the line.

....

“Let’s get cracking.”

JJ’s building supplies yard is where Bob buys his supplies. It’s always neat and tidy because JJ likes everything to be in its right place. JJ likes model planes and his pet parrot, Hamish.

“Think green!”

Molly is JJ’s daughter. She hires out the skips. Molly loves nature and she likes to “think green” and recycle as many things as she can. Molly likes music, too, but what she loves best of all is drawing and painting.

“Mustn’t dawdle, mustn’t dawdle.”

Skip is JJ’s delivery truck. There’s always lots for him to do, but sometimes he can’t stop himself daydreaming.

Skip

“Easy peasy.”

Trix is JJ’s forklift truck. She’s a hard worker, but she loves a good joke, too. She usually does what JJ asks her to – but not always!

Meet Bob's friends down on the farm

"Hello!"

Farmer Pickles runs a busy farm. He and Bob always try to help each other if they have tricky jobs to do. Farmer Pickles loves music and he's the leader of the local band.

"Ruff!"

Scruffty is Farmer Pickles' puppy. He's a happy-yappy waggy taily sort of pup who's always on the go. He loves burying things – especially bones! – and chasing rabbits.

"Travis Tractor is my name, moving loads is my game."

Travis is Farmer Pickles' tractor. He's very helpful, and he and his trailer come in handy for all sorts of jobs. He goes "ho, ho" when he laughs.

"Spud's on the job! Ha, ha!"

Spud is the farm scarecrow. It's his job to scare away the crows, but he'd rather spend his time playing tricks and telling jokes. Spud loves cake, and one day he'd like to be the first scarecrow in space.

"Caw!"

Squawk the crow likes making fun of Spud. He enjoys flying way up high, then dive-bombing him!

Roley's important job

Mr and Mrs Sabatini were looking at the plans for their new shop.

"Will it-a be-a biiiig enough?" asked Mrs Sabatini. "There's-a lot-a to fit in – it's-a lot of-a work."

"Don't worry, we can do it," said Bob. "I'll work with Wendy, and Scoop and Muck will clear the site. Dizzy will mix the plaster and Lofty will help with the shop window."

"What about me?" said Roley. "Is there any rolling for me to do?"

"Er, not really," said Bob.

"Oh, well, I'll come with you anyway," said Roley. "Just in case."

"Right, team," said Bob. "Let's get started."

"**Can we fix it?**" said Scoop.

"Yes we can!" said the others.

All except Lofty. "Er ... yeah ... I think so."

The first job was the shop front.

Lofty lifted out the old window.

Muck and Scoop put the bricks and rubble into Skip's skip.

Dizzy whizzed around, mixing cement in her mixer.

Roley wanted to help but there was nothing for him to do.

"I'll go back to the yard, Bob," he said sadly.

"OK, see you later," said Bob.

When Roley got back to the yard, Bird flew up on to his cab.

"Toot-toot?" he asked. He wondered what was wrong.

"Everybody's busy on Mr Sabatini's shop – except me," said Roley.

Just then Hamish, JJ's parrot, flew into the yard.

"Toot!" said Bird.

"TOOT!" said Hamish. He always copies what the others say.

Roley smiled. "That sounds like a song. Hey, let's make up a song for Mrs Sabatini's new shop."

"**New shop!**" said Hamish. He seemed to like the idea.

"**Toot!**" So did Bird.

Later, when Lofty rumbled into the yard, Roley, Hamish and Bird were singing their song.

"Now I'm telling you about this deli," sang Roley.

"**About this deli!**" squawked Hamish.

"**Toot, toot!**" sang Bird.

"It's better than anything on the telly!"

"**On the telly!**"

"**Toot, toot!**"

"What do you think, Lofty?" asked Roley.

"Well, it's quite good, but, er ... oh, I'm sure you'll get it right in the end," said Lofty.

"Right, come on, birdies," said Roley. "Try again. This song's got to be perfect."

Roley started again. "The Sabatinis are the grooviest team."

"**Grooviest team!**" squawked Hamish.

"**Toot, toot!**" said Bird.

Roley rolled his eyes. "No, no, nooooo!" he said. "It's just not right!"

Bird and Hamish looked at Roley. Then they looked at each other – and flew off!

"Oh, I'd better go and find them," said Roley.

He was rumbling through the town when he heard Mr Sabatini's violin. He heard Hamish and Bird, too.

"**Aaaark!**"

"**Toot!**"

Hamish and Bird didn't look pleased to see Roley.

"I know I was a bit horrible to

you," said Roley. "Sorry. You didn't do anything wrong. It's just that the song needs something. Something like ... Mr Sabatini's violin!"

The new shop was soon finished. Mrs Sabatini was filling it with all sorts of yummy things when Roley arrived with Bird, Hamish, Mr Sabatini – and his violin!

"Now I'm telling you about this deli," sang Roley.

"**About this deli!**" squawked Hamish.

"**Toot, toot!**" Bird whistled.

"It's better than anything on the telly."

"**On the telly!**"

"**Toot, toot!**"

"It ain't easy, I can tell you, man.

Who can make it happen? The Sabatinis can! Oh, oh, oh, y-eee-aaa-yyy!"

"**Oh, y-eee-aaa-yyy!**"

"**Toot, toot!**"

Bob, Wendy and Mrs Sabatini clapped.

"Is-a the best-a song I ever-a heard!" said Mrs Sabatini. "And is-a the best-a shop I ever-a saw!"

Bob smiled. "Thanks. We all had important jobs to do today. But I think Roley's was the MOST important!"

Roley grinned and rolled his eyes.

"Aww, thanks, Bob," said Roley.

"**Aww, thanks, Bob,**" said Hamish.

"**Toot, toot!**" said Bird.

A Bobsville picture puzzle

Which of these picture pieces will complete the big picture of Bobsville? You can draw and colour them in if you like.

ANSWER: Pieces 1, 2 and 6 will complete the puzzle.

Lofty the artist

1

Wendy was making some school library furniture for Mrs Percival. There were shelves and little tables and chairs. "The children will love them," said Bob.

2

Lofty picked up a chair with his grabber and took it to Molly. She was helping Wendy by painting all the new furniture in nice bright colours.

3

Lofty spotted some of Molly's paintings. "I've painted one of you, Lofty," said Molly. "I'll let you see it when I've finished painting all this furniture."

4

"I'd like to be an artist," said Lofty. He tried to pick up a big brush in his grabber, but he dropped it. "Ooo-er, it's very hard," he said. "I don't think I can do it."

5

"You can still help by lifting this air cooling unit," said Muck. "It blows out cold air when the weather is hot. We're going to fit it in Mr Sabatini's bistro to keep it cool."

6

Bob loaded bags of plaster on to Dizzy. "After Mr Sabatini's we'll get the wallpaper from JJ's and finish the library." Dizzy whizzed around. "Such a busy day!"

7

Bob nodded. "Yes, so let's get going," he said. "**Can we fix it?**" said Scoop. "**Yes we can!**" said the others. All except Lofty. "Er ... yeah ... I think so."

8

Bob and the team got to work. Lofty took the cooling unit to Mr Sabatini's bistro in his grabber. It didn't take Bob long to fix it to the wall.

9

"Now I-a need to paint the wall," said Mr Sabatini. "Use colours of foods," said Lofty. "Red for tomatoes and green for peppers." "Brilliant!" said Mr Sabatini.

10

Just then, Bob's mobile phone rang. "Could you go to JJ's to collect the wallpaper for the school library, Lofty?" asked Bob. "OK," said Lofty.

11

When Lofty got to JJ's yard Trix asked him why he looked sad. "I want to be an artist," said Lofty. "But I can't even hold a paintbrush properly. It's too hard!"

12

"Help me tidy the tins of paint and stacks of tiles instead, then," said Trix. "Right," said Lofty. "I'll put the red ones next to the yellow ones. Hey, this is good fun!"

13

"Lovely!" said Trix. "You're very artistic. But I'm fast!" She stacked bags of cement one on top of the other. But there were too many, and they fell on to the paint tins!

14

Just then, Mr Dixon arrived with the wallpaper. Lofty tried to stop the tins of paint rolling across the yard, but he ended up running over the rolls of wallpaper!

15

When Bob arrived Lofty said, "Look, the wallpaper's squashed! Oh, I'm so big and clumsy! I'll never be an artist." Bob smiled. "It was an accident, that's all."

16

Bob was helping Lofty and Trix to tidy up when JJ arrived. "Do you have any more wallpaper?" asked Lofty. "I do," said JJ. "But it's too dull for Mrs Percival."

17

Lofty had an idea! He poured paint from one of the tins on to the ground then drove through it. "Look," he said. "My wheels have made tyre-track patterns."

18

Lofty asked Bob to unroll some wallpaper on the ground. Then he drove through the different colours of paint and made patterns on the wallpaper. "Wow!" said Trix.

19

When the patterns were finished and the paint had dried, Bob, Lofty and Trix took the wallpaper to Mrs Percival. "It's not quite what you ordered," said Bob.

20

Mrs Percival unrolled the wallpaper. "It's delightful!" she said. "So bold and bright. Where did you get it?" Bob smiled and said, "It's a long story. I'll explain later."

21

Wendy got to work hanging the wallpaper. Then the team fitted the book shelves and furniture. "Isn't Lofty clever?" said Wendy. "He certainly is!" said Bob.

22

"The library looks fabulous," said Mrs Percival. "The wallpaper is wonderful!" Bob told her that Lofty had made the patterns on it. "He's a real artist!" she said.

23

Molly had a thank-you gift for Lofty. It was a painting of him! "It's called **Lofty the Artist**," she told him, "because you **are** an artist."

24

"Cool!" said Trix. "Brilliant!" said Muck. Lofty was very pleased. Very pleased indeed. "ME?" he said. "Lofty the Artist? Wow! Hee hee hee! Hee hee haa!"

Count with Bob
My team and I have lots and lots of tools and equipment! Can you help me sort them out? Count how many there are of each item then write your answers in the boxes.

ANSWER: a. 6 hammers; b. 2 brushes; c. 3 tins; d. 4 spanners; e. 5 saws; f. 1 drill.

Skip's big idea

Bob, Scoop and Skip were building a rockery in Mr Beasley's garden when Mr Bentley came to talk to Bob.

"The Mayor wants to put on an art exhibition the day after tomorrow," said Mr Bentley. "But there's nowhere big enough for it."

"What about the Old Mill?" said Scoop.

"It needs lots of repairs," said Mr Bentley.

"We can do those!" said Scoop.

Bob wasn't so sure. "It's a lot of work to do in a very short time," he said.

"I'll help," said Mr Beasley. "My rockery can wait. I think Scoop's idea is wonderful."

Skip looked a bit sad. "I wish I could have good ideas like Scoop," he whispered.

There were lots of jobs to do at the Old Mill.

"There's a big hole in one of the walls," said Bob.

"And lots of old plaster to get rid of," said Wendy. "I'll get started."

"Right. Come on, gang," said Bob.

"**Can we fix it?**" said Scoop.

"**Yes we can!**" said the others.

All except Lofty. "Er ... yeah ... I think so."

Bob had jobs for all the team.

"Roley, will you make a level base for the scaffolding? Then we'd better do something about this hole in the wall."

"I've got an idea!" said Skip. "Why don't we make the hole into a big doorway?"

"That's just what I planned to do," said Bob. "I've already ordered the door from JJ."

"Oh," said Skip.

"Muck and Scoop are clearing rubbish from inside. Why don't you take it to the dump with

Mr Beasley?" said Bob.

"Will do, Bob!" said Skip.

Scoop and Muck filled Skip's skip with rubble and he set off to the dump.

When the scaffolding was up, Bob attached a big tube to the top.

"What's that, Bob?" asked Roley.

"It's a rubble chute," Bob told him. "We can throw the bricks down it into Skip's skip next time."

Meanwhile, Skip's mind wasn't really on the job. "Must-have-an-idea," he said. "Must-have-an-idea."

When Skip passed Mrs Broadbent's house, there were all sorts of things outside.

"I'm getting rid of some old stuff," said Mrs Broadbent. "But I'm not sure what to do with it."

"I've got an idea!" said Skip. "We could take it to the dump for you." But then he remembered. "Oh, I can't. I'm doing an important job for Bob. Sorry."

When Skip got back to the Old Mill, he had another idea for Bob. "You could make a sort of chute and drop all the ..."

Then he saw the rubble chute. "Ah, you've already got one," he said.

Bob pushed rubble down the chute into Skip's skip and he set off on another trip to the dump.

On the way back, Mr Beasley saw some new ducks by the pond and got down to look at them.

"I think they're rare," said Mr Beasley.

But Skip wasn't listening. "If only I could have an idea," he said to himself. "Just one ..."

"Yes," said Mr Beasley. "I think they build ..."

"Did you just say 'build'?" said Skip. "Oh no, I've been so busy thinking that I forgot all about the job!" And with that he sped off – without Mr Beasley!

"Come back!" cried Mr Beasley.

When he got to the site, Skip

was going so fast that he couldn't stop, and he crashed into the scaffolding.

"Whoa!" said Bob. The scaffolding bent and Bob had to hold on. "Get me down!"

Skip had an idea! "In a minute!" he said, and he raced off to Mrs Broadbent's house.

"Have you come to take my old stuff away?" she asked.

"Just the mattress!" said Skip. "Can you put it in my skip, please?"

When Skip got back to the Old Mill, Bob was still hanging on to the scaffolding.

Skip stood at the bottom of the rubble chute. "Climb into the chute, Bob, then undo your harness," he said. "Don't worry, there's a soft mattress in my skip for you to land on."

"Here goes!" said Bob.

He landed safely and smiled at Skip.

"It was all my fault," said Skip.

"I was so busy trying to think of a good idea that I ..."

"But you **did** have a good idea, Skip," said Bob. "In fact you had a **brilliant** idea. It was your idea to use the chute and the mattress to get me down safely."

"Yes, I **did** have a good idea, didn't I?" said Skip.

Soon, the Old Mill was finished.

"You've done a splendid job, Bob," said Mr Bentley. "The Mayor is very pleased."

"Thanks," said Bob. "But I couldn't have done it without Wendy and the team – especially Skip. He was running from here to the dump, and ..."

"The dump!" cried Skip. "Oh, no, I forgot to take Mrs Broadbent's stuff to the dump!"

He zoomed off, leaving Mr Beasley behind again.

"Oh, no," said Mr Beasley. "Not again! Wait for me, Skip! Come back!"

Skip's picture puzzle

I've got another good idea, and this one's a puzzle for you to do! Can you draw lines to join sets of two pictures that are the same? Which one is left over? Draw it in the empty shape to complete the last pair.

ANSWER: The yellow Bob in the blue hat is left over.

Scoop the disco digger

 Jenny is staying with her sister  Wendy. "You

 and  Bob need a holiday," says  Jenny.

"Where would you like to go?"

 Wendy shakes her head. "We're too busy,"

she says. When  Wendy goes into the

office  Scoop says, "I've got an idea. Let's

make a holiday for  Bob and  Wendy!"

 Roley is puzzled. "How?" he asks.

"We can use sand to make a beach and

do dancing and stuff," says  Scoop.

"  Scoop can be the Disco Digger!"

says Jenny. Just then  Bob and

 Wendy come into the yard. "What's

going on?" asks  Bob. "Nothing,  Bob,"

says  Dizzy. "No, nothing at all, Bob,"

says Roley. "Right," says  Bob.

"We have to mend some old water

pipes today so we'd better get going."

"**Can we fix it?**" says  Scoop.

"**Yes we can!**" say the others. All

except  Lofty. "Er ... yeah ... I think so."

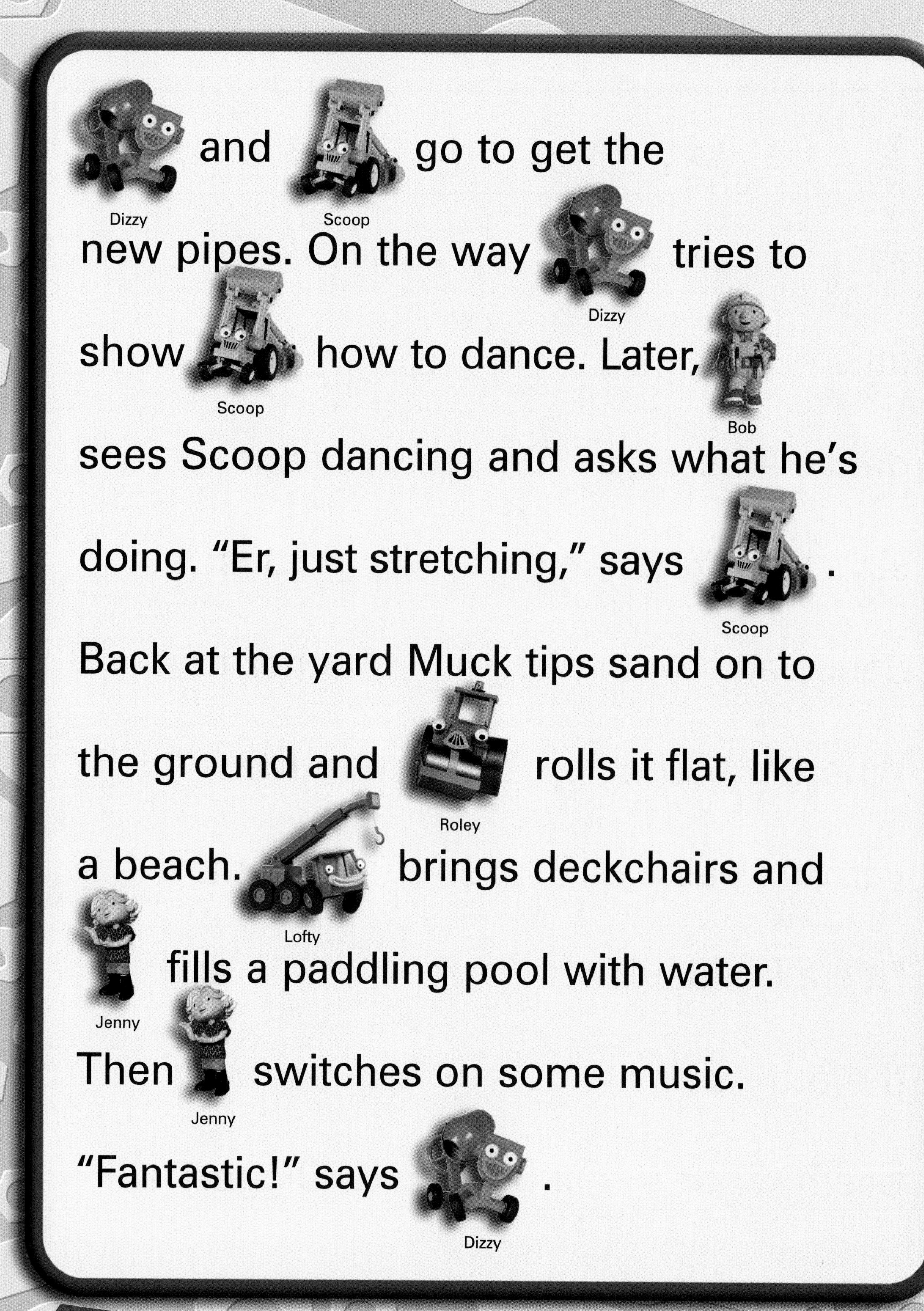

and go to get the
Dizzy Scoop

new pipes. On the way tries to
Dizzy

show how to dance. Later,
Scoop Bob

sees Scoop dancing and asks what he's

doing. "Er, just stretching," says .
Scoop

Back at the yard Muck tips sand on to

the ground and rolls it flat, like
Roley

a beach. brings deckchairs and
Lofty

fills a paddling pool with water.
Jenny

Then switches on some music.
Jenny

"Fantastic!" says .
Dizzy

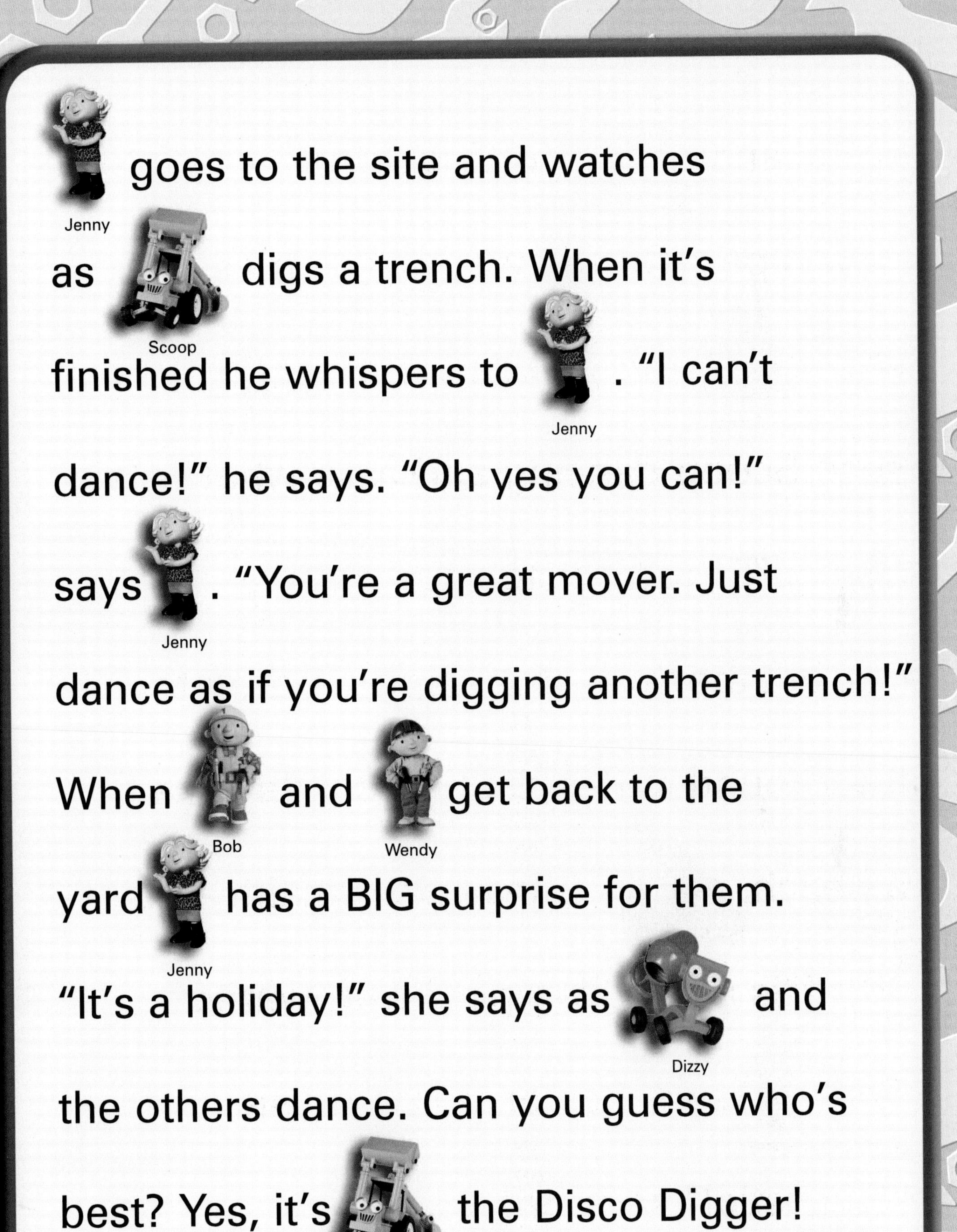

Jenny goes to the site and watches as Scoop digs a trench. When it's finished he whispers to Jenny. "I can't dance!" he says. "Oh yes you can!" says Jenny. "You're a great mover. Just dance as if you're digging another trench!"

When Bob and Wendy get back to the yard Jenny has a BIG surprise for them. "It's a holiday!" she says as Dizzy and the others dance. Can you guess who's best? Yes, it's Scoop the Disco Digger!

Busy Bobsville

Bobsville is a very busy place! Can you find Bob and his friends in the big picture? Tick a box for each one you find, and say their names.

Mr Bentley's winter fair

1

Bob and his team were getting things ready for the Bobsville winter fair. "There are lots of stalls to sort out, so we'd better get going," said Bob.

2

Mr Bentley had to make sure all the jobs got done. Bob spoke to him on his walkie-talkie. "Yes, we're on our way," he said. "Over and out."

3

The winter fair was going to be in the Town Hall Square. There were lots of people there already by the time Bob and the team arrived.

4

Mr Bentley showed them a big map with all the stalls marked on it. "Mrs Percival's stall is to be moved, Mr Ellis wants a bigger stall and ..."

5

Mr Bentley took a breath. "But perhaps you could start with the Christmas lights, Bob. And don't forget the big blow-up Santa, will you?"

6

Farmer Pickles and Travis arrived with Humphrey the pig for the "Guess the weight of the pig" competition. Mr Bentley ticked his name.

7

Wendy was helping Bob with the Christmas lights. "There's a lot for Mr Bentley to organise," she said. "I hope he hasn't given himself too much to do."

8

Pam Goody wanted her plant stall moved. "I'll get it done right away," said Mr Bentley. Spud was right behind him. "Right away!" said Spud. "Leave it to me."

9

Mr Bentley went to check on Humphrey. "His pen is in the wrong place!" he said. "And the gate's not safe. That's another job for Bob. I'll go and find him."

10

Spud sat down beside the pig pen to eat a slice of pizza. Cheeky Humphrey pushed open the gate, snatched the pizza – and ran off with it! "Oi!" said Spud.

11

Wendy fitted the blow-up Santa to a pump, and he slowly filled with air. "We're blowing Santa up now, Mr Bentley," Bob said into his walkie-talkie.

12

Soon Santa was bobbing and bouncing around in front of the town hall. "Make sure you hold on to the rope, Wendy!" said Bob. "I'm trying, Bob!" said Wendy.

13

Mr Bentley took one of the ropes but Santa bobbed around, and kicked his bottom! Then Spud and Humphrey ran past. "Make way for pig and scarecrow!" cried Spud.

14

Humphrey bumped into Mr Bentley and the aerial of his walkie-talkie made a hole in the blow-up Santa. PSSSSTT! All the air escaped, and Santa flopped on to the ground.

15

Humphrey was still on the run. Spud was right behind him but he just couldn't catch him. "**OINK, OINK!**" said Humphrey, running past Mrs Potts' knitting stall.

16

"**OINK!**" said Humphrey as he knocked over Mrs Percival. The pottery on her stall crashed to the ground. Then Humphrey bashed into JJ's DIY stall.

17

When he smelled Mr Sabatini's pizzas, Humphrey ran to his stall. He knocked the pizzas to the ground and began eating them. "Oh, is-a disaster!" said Mr Sabatini.

18

"What a mess!" said Mr Bentley. "The winter fair is ruined, and it's all my fault!" Bob looked around. "Don't worry," he said. "If we all work together we can fix it."

19

Bob was right. Everyone helped. First Spud got Humphrey back into his pen with the help of another slice of Mr Sabatini's pizza. "Well done!" said Mr Bentley.

20

Then Wendy got to work. She fixed the broken leg on Mrs Potts' wool stall. Then she mended JJ's stall. "That's jobs two and three done!" said Mr Bentley.

21

Next, Wendy fitted a bright yellow roof on Molly's arts and crafts stall. "Wonderful, Wendy!" said Mr Bentley as he ticked off one more job on his list.

22

Bob and Wendy patched up the blow-up Santa and blew him up again. Soon all the jobs were done. "That's everything!" said Mr Bentley, ticking his list.

23

Everyone had a wonderful time at the winter fair. "Thank you all," said Mr Bentley. "I couldn't have done it without your help. Thanks to all of you – even Spud!"

24

Just then, the Mayor spoke to Mr Bentley on his walkie-talkie. He looked a bit worried. "What is it?" asked Bob. "She wants me to do another winter fair next year!"

Snowed under

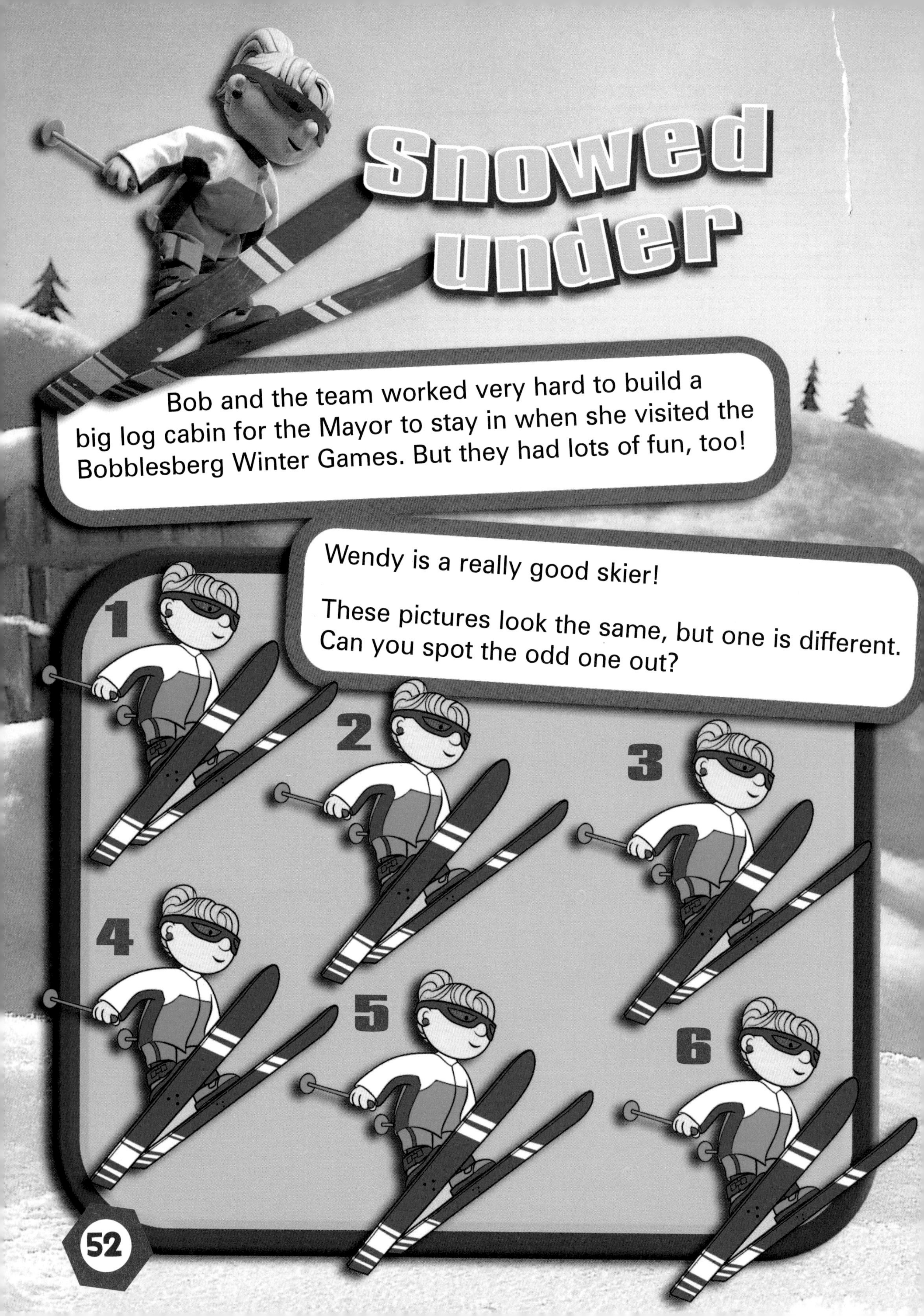

Bob and the team worked very hard to build a big log cabin for the Mayor to stay in when she visited the Bobblesberg Winter Games. But they had lots of fun, too!

Wendy is a really good skier!

These pictures look the same, but one is different. Can you spot the odd one out?

1
Zoom! When he had some time off, Bob loved riding around on Zoomer the snowmobile. He's VERY fast!
2
Look carefully at these 2 pictures. Can you spot 5 things that have changed colour in picture 2?
ANSWERS: Picture 3 is the odd one out. The 5 things that have changed colour are Bob's goggles and jumper, the splash of snow, and Zoomer's nostril and mouth.

Trix's pumpkin pie

JJ's building supplies yard is usually a busy place, but one day Trix had nothing to do.

"Skip's at the dump with Molly," she told JJ. "Have you got a job for me to do?"

JJ pointed to a big bag of wood chippings. "You can take those chippings to Bob for me," he said. "He's building a climbing frame in the school playground."

Trix scooped up the bag on her fork and set off.

When she got to the school, Bob and the team were marking out an area for the climbing frame.

"What are the chippings for?" asked Trix.

"We're going to put them under the climbing frame," said Bob. "If any of the children fall off they'll land on something soft."

When Bob asked Muck to go to Farmer Pickles' farm to pick up the wooden poles for the climbing frame, Trix asked if she could go with him.

"Of course you can!" said Muck.

When they got to the farm Farmer Pickles had some big pumpkins in Travis' trailer.

"What are those?" asked Trix.

"They're pumpkins," said Farmer Pickles. "I'm going to sell them at the market."

Two pumpkins were left in a wheelbarrow. "What about those two?" asked Trix.

"One's going into a pumpkin pie for the Harvest Supper tonight," said Farmer Pickles. "And the other one is for a SURPRISE!"

"Are you going to bake the pie?" asked Muck.

"No," said Farmer Pickles. "Mrs Percival's going to bake it in

Mr Sabatini's big pizza oven. Which reminds me, I really need to get it there ..."

"I'll take it AND the poles!" said Trix.

After she had delivered the poles to the school, Trix raced off into town with the pumpkin.

Mrs Percival was very pleased with it.

"Eeet will make-a the beeeegest-a pie in the world!" said Mr Sabatini. "Why not-a stay and watch, Treeeex?"

"I can't," said Trix. "I've got so much to do today!"

When Trix got back to the school, Bob and the team had built part of the frame.

Trix helped move the poles.

Muck helped with the tyres and ropes.

Lofty lifted up the roof.

The last job was to spread out

the wood chippings under the frame. But there weren't enough.

"I'll get another bag!" said Trix.

When Trix passed Mr Sabatini's pizza parlour on the way to JJ's, Mrs Percival was standing outside with a HUGE pumpkin pie.

"I'll take it to Farmer Pickles for you," said Trix.

On the way, Trix met Spud. "I'm taking this pie to Farmer Pickles," she told him. "But I've got to take Bob a bag of chippings, too. I don't know which job to do first!"

Spud looked at the pie, sniffed – and grinned. "Leave the pie with me, Trix," he said. "I'll look after it for you."

"Oh, thank you!" said Trix.

Later on, when Mrs Percival told Wendy that Trix had taken the pie to the farm she frowned. "I don't think Trix can do two jobs at once," she said. "I'll go and help."

Wendy arrived at JJ's yard at the same time as Trix, who looked very hot and bothered.

"I'm in a bit of a muddle, Wendy," said Trix. "I was taking the pie to the farm, but then I remembered the chippings, so I left the pie with Spud and ..."

"SPUD?" cried Wendy. "He LOVES pie! He'll eat it!"

"Oh, no!" cried Trix. "I've got to stop him!"

"I'll come with you," said Wendy.

Spud was just about to take a bite of the pumpkin pie when Squawk and the other crows arrived.

"**Ark! Ark!**" they crowed. They wanted some pie, too!

Spud waved his arms around. "Oi, shoo! Get off my pie!" he cried.

He was still trying to scare the crows away when Wendy and Trix arrived.

Trix scooped the pie on to her fork and set off to the farm.

Spud watched her go. "Oh, no, my lovely pie ..."

That night, at the Harvest Supper, Farmer Pickles showed everyone his surprise. He had carved a face on the big pumpkin and put lights inside.

"Yippee!" said Trix. "It's a lovely lantern!"

Mrs Percival cut the first piece of pumpkin pie and gave it to – Spud!

"You deserve it," said Trix. "There wouldn't BE any pie if you hadn't looked after it for me. You're a hero!"

Munch! Spud took a big bite of pie.

"I suppose I am a hero!" he said. "Spud the hero!" **Munch!**

"Is there any more pie, Mrs Percival?"

Paint with Molly

When she isn't working, Molly just loves drawing and painting. One day she got out her easel and paints and looked around the yard. "What shall I paint today, Dad?" she asked JJ. "Shall I draw your picture?" Before he had a chance to reply, up zoomed Trix the forklift truck. "Draw me, draw me!" said Trix. "Please?" So Molly did!

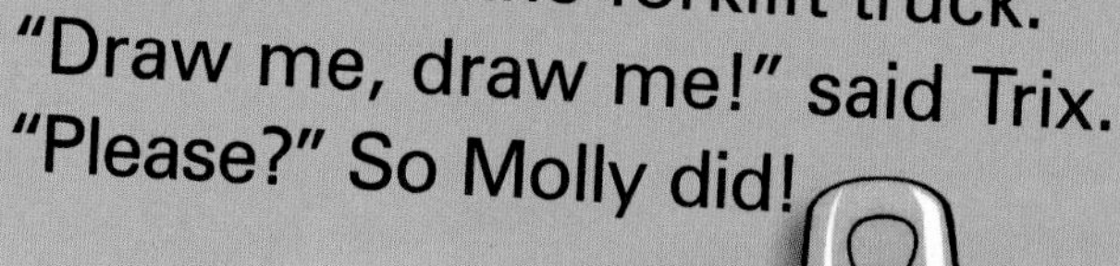

Trix by Molly

Trix by ____________________

Why not colour in Molly's drawing of Trix? The spots of colour will show you which colours to use. When your picture is finished, write your name on the line above.

Pilchard and the fieldmice

1

Bob and the team were going to put in a new beam at Mr Ellis' cottage. Pilchard jumped on to a workbench. "**Miaow?**" she said. "No, you can't come!" said Bob.

2

Bob jumped on to Muck. "Let's get going," he said. "**Can we fix it?**" said Scoop. "**Yes we can!**" said the others. All except Lofty. "Er ... yeah ... I think so."

3

Bob and Muck led the team out of the yard. What they didn't know was that Pilchard had jumped into Muck's back dumper. She was determined to go with them.

4

At JJ's, Muck lowered his dumper so that Trix could put some things in it. "**MIAOW!**" Pilchard almost fell out! Bob picked her up and said, "You're going back to the yard!"

5

When they got back to the yard, Bob put Pilchard down. "Now you stay here," he told her, and the team set off to Mr Ellis'. But naughty Pilchard followed them!

6

Bob was in Mr Ellis' garden working out how he was going to cut the beam when three little fieldmice scurried towards him. Bob didn't see them.

7

But Pilchard did! "**Miaow!**" she purred. She sneaked towards them and was just about to pounce when Mr Ellis arrived with tea and biscuits. Pilchard had to hide!

8

Bob decided to save one of his biscuits for later so he put it on the beam. When the fieldmice started to nibble at it, Pilchard jumped out at them. "**Miaow!**"

9

"What are you doing here?" said Bob. "It's dangerous. You'll have to stay indoors where it's safe." Pilchard didn't like that! She sat in the window and cried, "**Yeowl!**"

10

When the beam was cut, Bob decided to eat his biscuit. But it had gone! The fieldmice had run off with it and taken it into the cottage through a hole in the door.

11

Pilchard could hardly believe her luck! She chased the fieldmice across the room, but they ran under the sofa where she couldn't get them. "**Eeek! EeeK!**"

12

When Bob and Dizzy went into the cottage to fix the beam, Pilchard was scratching at the sofa. Bob picked her up. "Out you go!" he said.

13

Bob got things ready so that he could take out the old beam. Outside, Pilchard howled and yowled. "I don't know what's wrong with that cat today!" said Bob.

14

Bob wasn't the only one who was busy. Down behind the sofa, the fieldmice were nibbling at his chocolate biscuit! **Nibble, nibble, nibble. "Eeek, eek, eek!"**

15

The fieldmice ran away when Bob went behind the sofa to plug in his power saw. He saw something by the plug. "It's my biscuit!" he said. "How did it get in here?"

16

When Wendy and Scoop arrived Wendy opened the door and Pilchard rushed inside. She ran round and round, looking for the fieldmice. "**Miaow! MIAOW!**"

17

Pilchard scratched at the sofa and the fieldmice scurried towards the front door. "Mice!" said Bob. "So that's what's been bothering Pilchard all day!"

18

Outside, the fieldmice jumped into Muck's shovel he lifted it up into the air. "Got them!" he cried. "You can take them to Farmer Pickles' farm later," said Bob.

19

Bob and Wendy worked hard, and soon they had taken out Mr Ellis' old beam and fitted the new one in its place. They were very pleased with it – and so was Mr Ellis.

20

Mr Ellis was pleased with Pilchard, too. "She got rid of the mice for me," he said to Bob, "so I've got her a little thank-you present. It's a clockwork mouse for her to play with."

21

Mr Ellis wound up the clockwork mouse and put it on the ground. It **whizzed, whirred** – then raced off across the grass. Pilchard was right behind it! "**Yeee-owl!**" she purred. This was even more fun than chasing real mice! Bob laughed. "Thanks, Mr Ellis," he said. "You've just made Pilchard a very happy cat!"

What do you know about me and my team? Try this fun quiz to find out! Look back through the book to help you.

1 What did we build for the Bobblesberg Winter Games? Was it:

a a ski jump

b an igloo or

c a log cabin?

2 What is the name of Farmer Pickles' puppy?

3 What was in the pie at Farmer Pickles' Harvest Supper?

4 What is JJ's daughter called? Is her name:

a Milly

b Molly or

c Polly?

5
Which machine is the leader of my team?

6
What is the name of JJ's pet parrot?

7
Who was in charge of the Bobsville winter fair?

8
What is the name of Farmer Pickles' pig? Is it:

a Humphrey

b Humpty Dumpty or

c Henry?

9
Which member of my team is a blue mobile crane?

10
What did Mr Ellis give Pilchard as a thank-you gift for getting rid of the fieldmice?

ANSWERS: 1. c, a log cabin; 2. Scruffty; 3. pumpkin; 4. b, Molly; 5. Scoop; 6. Hamish; 7. Mr Bentley; 8. a, Humphrey; 9. Lofty; 10. a clockwork mouse.